This Little Tiger book belongs to:

_____

_____

_____

For Anna
– S S

To Mum, Dad and his delicious vegetable soup
– J D

LITTLE TIGER PRESS LTD
an imprint of the Little Tiger Group
1 Coda Studios
189 Munster Road, London SW6 6AW
www.littletiger.co.uk

First published in Great Britain 2006
This edition published 2018

Text copyright © Steve Smallman 2006
Illustrations copyright © Joëlle Dreidemy 2006
Steve Smallman and Joëlle Dreidemy have asserted their
rights to be identified as the author and illustrator of this
work under the Copyright, Designs and Patents Act, 1988

A CIP catalogue record for this book
is available from the British Library
All rights reserved

ISBN 978-1-78881-040-1
LTP/1800/2260/0218
Printed in China
10 9 8 7 6 5 4 3 2 1

THE LAMB WHO CAME FOR DINNER

STEVE SMALLMAN   JOËLLE DREIDEMY

LITTLE TIGER
LONDON

"Vegetable soup AGAIN!"
moaned the old wolf. "Oh,
I wish I had a little lamb.
I could make a hotpot,
my favourite!"
    Just then . . . .

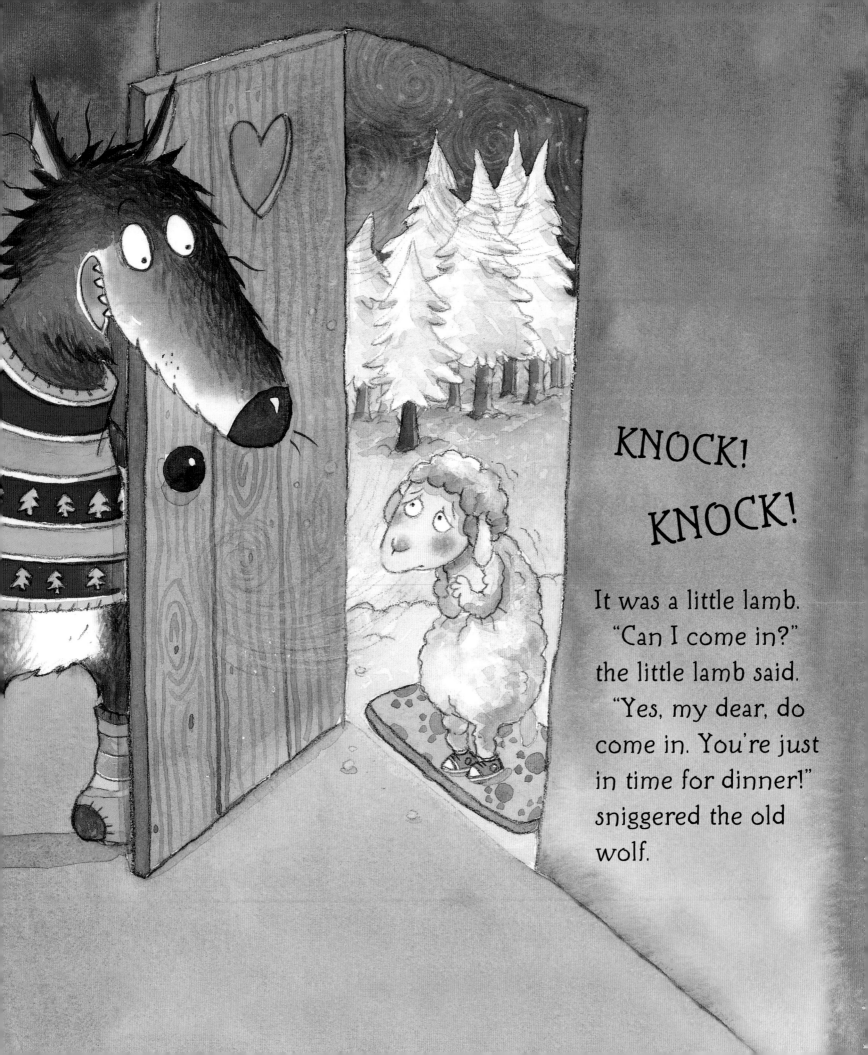

KNOCK!
KNOCK!

It was a little lamb.
"Can I come in?"
the little lamb said.
"Yes, my dear, do
come in. You're just
in time for dinner!"
sniggered the old
wolf.

The little lamb was shivering
with cold.
BRRRR! BRRRR! she went.
"GOODNESS GRACIOUS ME!"
said the old wolf. "I can't eat
a lamb that's frozen. I HATE
frozen food!"
So he put her next to the
fire to thaw her out.

The old wolf looked up
a recipe for lamb hotpot.
Mmmmmm! He felt hungry
just at the thought of it.

The lamb was feeling hungry
too. Her tummy rumbled.
RUMBLE! RUMBLE! it went.
   "GOODNESS GRACIOUS ME!"
said the old wolf. "I can't eat a
lamb with a rumbling tummy.
I might get indigestion!"

So he gave the lamb
a carrot to eat. "Stuffing,"
he said to himself.

The little lamb gobbled
down the carrot so quickly
that she got hiccups!

HIC,
HIC,
HICCUP!

she went.

"GOODNESS GRACIOUS
ME!" said the old wolf.
"I can't eat a lamb with
hiccups! I might catch
them too!"
    But he didn't know
how to cure hiccups.

He tried throwing the
lamb up in the air.

HIC!

That didn't work.

He held her
upside-down.

HIC!

That didn't work.

He twirled her
round and round.

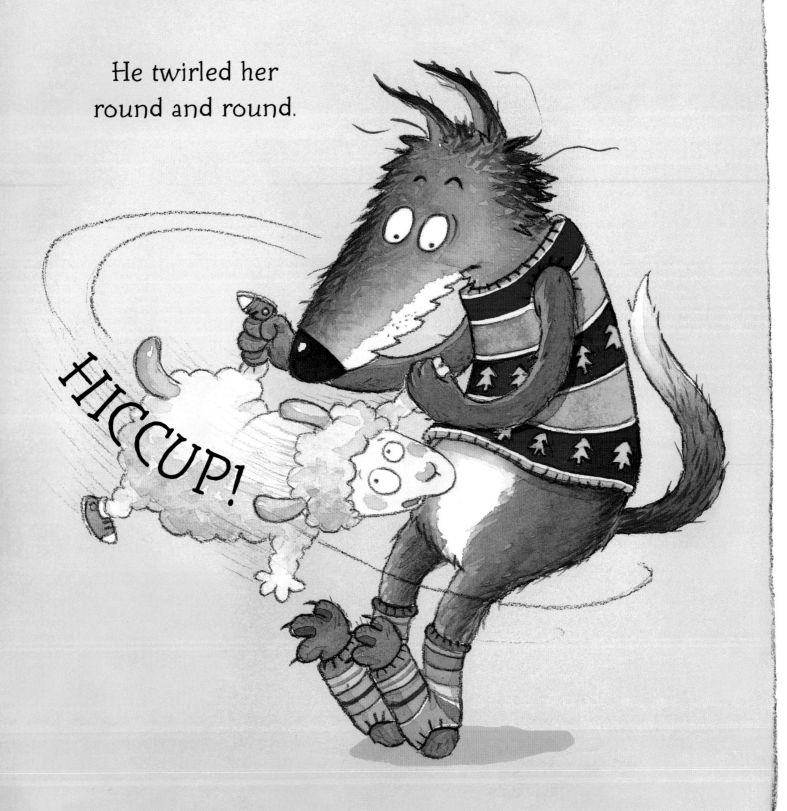

HICCUP!

That didn't work either!

So the old wolf put the lamb over
his shoulder and patted her back with
his big hairy paw.

The lamb stopped hiccupping, snuggled
under the old wolf's shaggy chin and fell
fast asleep in his arms. The old wolf felt
funny. He'd never been hugged by his
dinner before and suddenly he didn't feel
so hungry after all.

The little lamb snored gently in his ear.
SNORE! SNORE! she went.

"Goodness gracious me!" whispered the
old wolf. "I can't eat a lamb that's snoring!"

He sniffed, then sniffed again. The little lamb smelt so . . . so . . . DELICIOUS! "Oh!" groaned the wolf. "If I eat her quickly, it'll be all right." And he was just about to gobble her up when . . .

The old wolf sat down in the chair by the fire, the little lamb warm on his chest, and thought just how very long it had been since anyone had given him a cuddle.

. . . she woke up and gave him a great big kiss.

SMACK!

"NOOO!!!"

howled the wolf, "THAT'S NOT FAIR! I am a big, bad WOLF and you are . . . hotpot!"

"Hop-pop!" said the little lamb with a smile. Then she pointed at the old wolf and said, "Woof!"

"Oh, give me strength!" groaned the old wolf. "You'll have to go!"

He wrapped the little lamb up warmly and put her outside.

"NOW GO AWAY!"

he shouted. "If you stay here, I'll eat you, and then we'll both be sorry!" And he shut the door with a

BANG!

It was dark outside, and cold.
The little lamb banged on the door.
  "Woof?" she cried. "Can I come in, Woof?"
  But the old wolf stuck his fingers in his ears
and went "LA! LA! LA!" until she stopped.
  At last, all was quiet. "Thank goodness she's gone!"
thought the wolf. "She's not safe here with
a hungry old wolf like me."

Then he thought of
the lamb, all alone in
the dark wood.

"She might get lost!"

"She might get frozen!"

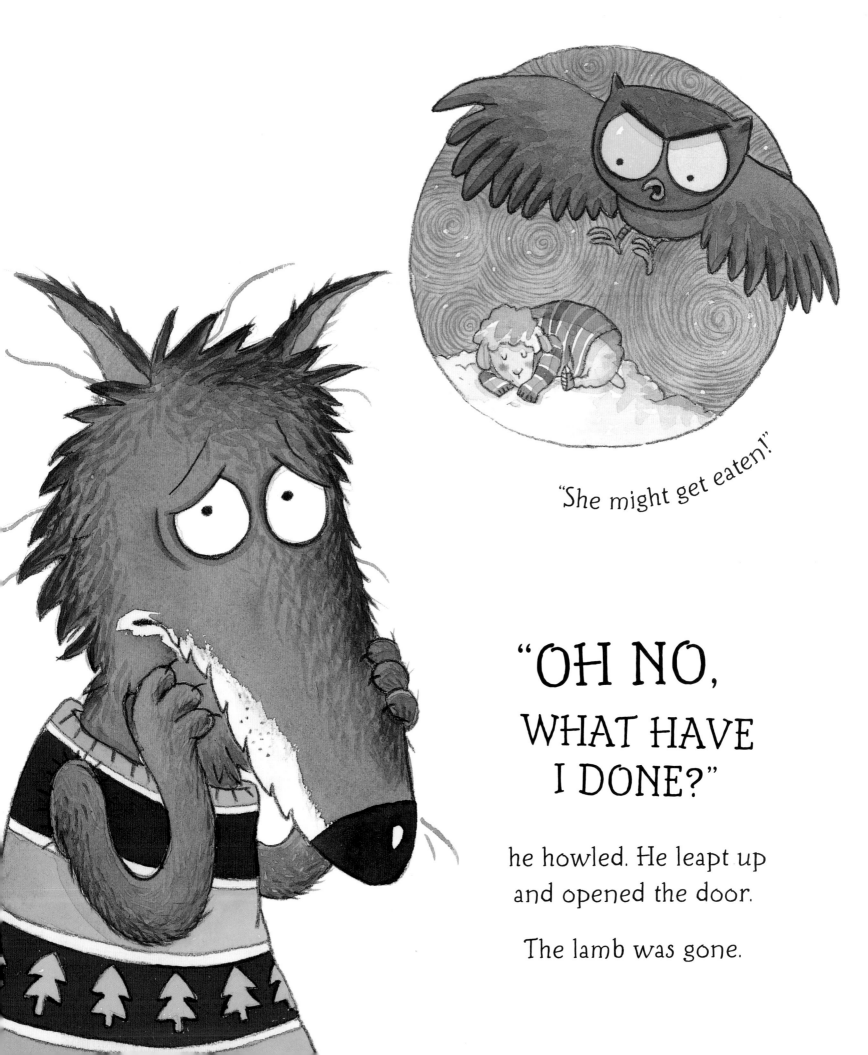

"She might get eaten!"

"OH NO,
WHAT HAVE
I DONE?"

he howled. He leapt up
and opened the door.

The lamb was gone.

The old wolf rushed out into the
dark wood, crying, "Little lamb!
Little lamb! Come back!
I won't eat you . . . I promise!"

Much, much later, a sad, soggy old wolf trudged wearily back to his cottage alone.

He pushed open the door and there, by the fire,
sat the little lamb!

"YOU CAME BACK!" said the wolf with
a smile. "Haven't you got anywhere else to go?"

The little lamb shook her head.

"Er . . . er . . . then would you like to
stay here . . . with me?" asked the wolf.

The little lamb gave him a hard stare.
"Not eat me, Woof, no?" she said.

"GOODNESS GRACIOUS ME!" said
the old wolf. "I can't eat a lamb
who needs me! I might
get heartburn!"

The little lamb
smiled and then
threw herself
into the old
wolf's arms.

"Are you feeling hungry,
Hotpot?" asked the wolf.

"How about some vegetable soup?

It's my favourite."

More fabulous books from Little Tiger Press!

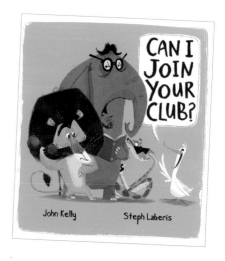

For information regarding any of the above books or for our catalogue, please contact us:
Little Tiger Press, 1 Coda Studios, 189 Munster Road, London SW6 6AW
Tel: 020 7385 6333 • E-mail: contact@littletiger.co.uk • www.littletiger.co.uk